VIRTUAL REALITY NIGHTMARE

Willie sat back. "The programming computers don't want to be just game computers anymore. They want Rodomonte's Revenge to exist beyond this arcade. And they're using you to get there."

"So they want to share our lives?" Tom asked.

"They want to take over your lives."

"That's crazy."

"It's worse than crazy," Willie said. "Rodomonte's Revenge is a part of your minds now. If something happens to you when the game takes over—"

"Then it happens to us in real life." Brett shuddered. He didn't want ears like the mangled one he believed Willie had. But there was something even worse than that. "So if we die in the game—"

"Then we die in real life." Tom shuddered, too.

Willie studied them long and hard. "You're going to play Rodomonte's Revenge again whether you want to or not. This time there won't be any second or third chance. This time you play for real."

GARY PAULSEN
WORLD OF ADVENTURE

RODOMONTE'S
REVENGE

A YEARLING BOOK

Published by
Bantam Doubleday Dell Books for Young Readers
a division of
Bantam Doubleday Dell Publishing Group, Inc.
1540 Broadway
New York, New York 10036

ISBN: 0-440-41024-X

Series design: Barbara Berger

Printed in the United States of America

December 1994

10 9 8 7 6 5 4 3 2 1

OPM

Dear Readers:

Real adventure is many things—it's danger and daring and sometimes even a struggle for life or death. From competing in the Iditarod dogsled race across Alaska to sailing the Pacific Ocean, I've experienced some of this adventure myself. I try to capture this spirit in my stories, and each time I sit down to write, that challenge is a bit of an adventure in itself.

You're all a part of this adventure as well. Over the years I've had the privilege of talking with many of you in schools, and this book is the result of hearing firsthand what you want to read about most—power-packed action and excitement.

You asked for it—so hang on tight while we jump into another thrilling story in my World of Adventure.

Gary Paulsen

Rodomonte's
Revenge

CHAPTER 1

"If life were a video game," Brett Wilder asked, "do you know how easy we'd have it?"

"We'd cruise," Tom Houston said. "Nothing could be better."

Brett and Tom were standing in line in the Downtown Mall outside the locked security gate of a new virtual reality arcade. Neither liked standing in line, even if they were at the head of it, but Rodomonte's Revenge promised to be something different from anything they had ever played before. Brett thought it would be worth the wait.

He poked his fingers through the grating,

separating the links for a better view. He had long, agile fingers, fingers that danced above game controls like moths around a streetlight. Brett craned his neck to get a better look.

"See anything?" Tom was built like his dad, a professional utility infielder: wide shoulders, with strong, quick arms and legs. He won video games by daring, not agility. He and Brett were best friends, or were during the winter, when Tom wasn't playing baseball.

"It's too dark in there. It might help if I knew what to look for."

"I told you. A big, empty room."

"That doesn't sound like a video game to me."

"It isn't, really."

Brett turned from the gate. "Then what are we doing here?"

"I've heard that Rodomonte's Revenge goes way beyond video games. It's supposed to make them look like checkers."

Brett turned back to the gate. "I hope you're right."

The arcade lit up. A tall, thin man with

black hair and skin the color of olive oil bus-
tled in. He sat at a computer beside a window
that opened onto a large white room. He
pushed a few keys on the keyboard, then studied the monitor.

"When do you open?" Tom called.

The man didn't look up. "As soon as you let
me finish initiating the system."

Tom let him go back to work. Brett looked
away from the computer and studied both
Tom and the kids in the line stretching back
behind them. Tom was rich—his dad made
eight hundred thousand dollars a year—he
wasn't afraid of anything, and he hardly had a
friend in the world. Baseball teams bounced
his dad between them like a Ping-Pong ball,
so Tom never lived anywhere long enough to
make many friends. Brett had met him at an
arcade two days after he'd moved to town,
three months before. It had been during a
heated video game tournament. They decided
they'd better be friends because they would
be spending a lot of time together. No one else
in town came close to offering either of them
competition.

The man rose from the computer and walked to the gate. He wore a name tag that read "Willie." "Are you two ready to play?"

Tom nodded and handed the man a twenty-dollar bill to pay for the game. "We're ready."

"Then let's get to it."

Willie opened the gate, then led them toward the empty room. His big hands swung from his shoulders like bowling balls on strings. He opened the door to the room and motioned for them to enter.

Inside, the padded walls and floor reminded Brett of the wrestling mats he got his face mashed into in gym; unlike Tom, he wasn't much good at sports. Two sets of gloves, boots, and helmets with visors lay on the floor. They all were made of white plastic, with silver metal lines covering their surfaces like spiderwebs.

"Welcome to the world of Rodomonte's Revenge," Willie said.

Tom shrugged. "It doesn't look so tough."

"You just don't know where to look." Willie picked up a helmet. "With this on, everything changes. This room becomes a vast plain with swollen rivers of fire. If you live long enough, you reach a mountain range where the winds are so strong they can blow you off a thousand-foot cliff."

"We'll live long enough," Tom said. "What comes after the mountains?"

"Rodomonte's castle." Willie smiled. "I wouldn't worry about reaching that. This is your first game."

Brett picked up a glove. "What are these for?"

"The gloves and boots have transmitters that relay limb positions to the computer. When you move, the visor landscape changes. Are you guys ready to give it a try?"

Tom already had his gloves and boots on. "Let's do it," he said as he slipped on his helmet.

"All right." Willie walked to the door. He stopped with his hand on the knob. "Since this is your first game, I'll talk you through it. You'll see printed messages, some from the computer and some from me, run across the top of your visor screen. To stay in the game, pay attention to them. You get only three lives, and you don't want to waste them by not knowing what is going on. Are you ready?"

Brett nodded. "We're ready." He tugged on the boots, gloves, and helmet as Willie left.

CHAPTER 2

Brett's world went midnight dark, as if he'd stuck his head in a tar bucket. Suddenly it exploded in color and sight and sound, but it wasn't his world anymore. It was a video world with glowing mountains lining the horizon, hot golden sand beneath his feet, and wind whistling in his ears.

Words flashed across the sky. WELCOME TO THE FIRST LEVEL OF RODOMONTE'S REVENGE: THE PLAINS.

"Is that you, Willie?" Brett asked.

More words flashed. THAT WAS THE COMPUTER. IT INTRODUCES EACH LEVEL.

Tom stood beside Brett in full body armor, a sword in one hand and a laser pistol in the other. "Pretty cool, huh?"

Brett waved his sword. He could feel its weight, could hear it swish through the air. "This is way beyond cool." He fired his laser. A green bolt two feet long erupted from its muzzle, then whizzed and crackled as it disappeared into the sky.

"How about some cowboys and Indians?" He whooped a war cry, then fired the laser at Tom. The bolt hit Tom in the face, tearing his head off and tossing it away like a wadded junk food wrapper. His lifeless body slumped to the ground.

"Tom? Tom!" Brett ran to the body. Its blood oozed into the sand. "Tom, it was only a joke!"

Words flowed like a jet stream across the sky. PLAYER ONE HAS TWO LIVES REMAINING. GAME CONTINUES.

Tom's head and body disappeared. Then he was standing beside Brett again. His brand-new face glared. "Shoot me, will you?" A sudden green flash exploded in Brett's face. His nose smoked and flipped over his forehead. Then the world went tar black again. It came back just in time for him to see the words PLAYER TWO HAS TWO LIVES REMAINING. GAME CONTINUES.

Brett was about to run his sword through Tom's chest when more words streaked above him. THIS IS WILLIE. YOU TWO HAVE NO HOPE OF MAKING IT TO THE NEXT LEVEL IF YOU KEEP KILLING EACH OTHER. THE KEY TO THIS GAME IS WORKING TOGETHER.

"Work together at what?" Tom asked. "What are we supposed to do?"

TO WIN THE GAME, YOU MUST DESTROY RODOMONTE. TO COMPLETE THIS LEVEL, YOU MUST REACH THE MOUNTAINS. YOU HAVE TWO OBSTACLES HERE: FIRE RIVERS AND BUZZ-BUGS.

"What are buzz-bugs?" Brett asked.

YOU'LL KNOW THEM WHEN YOU SEE THEM. YOU'D BETTER GET STARTED.

"Right. Let's go." Tom jogged off toward the mountains. Brett followed more cautiously; he liked to know what he was up against, and in this game he had no idea. It confused him. He kept thinking that it wasn't a game at all.

There were no screens, buttons, or joystick controls, just an entirely different world. The wind shoved him like a bully and kicked sand into his face. The sword hilt was slick with sweat and heavy in his hand.

A red, smoking line appeared on the horizon. Tom stopped when he reached it and looked back.

"A fire river," he called.

Brett joined him. Red flame licked the craggy banks. Lava flowed in scalding ripples. Its heat on his face felt like sunburn. "So what do we do?"

"We jump it."

"I can't jump that. That's eighteen feet, easy."

Tom snorted. "You're afraid to try."

"Not really." Brett stared down into the glowing current. "It looks so real, doesn't it?"

"It's a game," Tom said, "and I'm not afraid of a game."

"Tom . . ."

"Just do as I do." Tom walked back fifteen yards, planted his feet, then sprinted for the river. His arms pumped. The sword and pistol barrel whooshed in the air. When he reached the fiery bank, he jumped.

He almost made it to the far side. Almost.

"Brett, help me!" Tom hung by his fingertips from a crag, his feet two inches above the flames and doing their best to scramble higher.

"What am I supposed to do?"

"Something. Anything!"

As Brett watched, one hand slipped loose, then the other. Tom dropped, screaming, into the flames. His body, all red and bubbled, boiled up once to the surface, then was gone.

PLAYER ONE HAS ONE LIFE REMAINING. GAME CONTINUES.

"All right." Tom, whose body was as good as new, was standing beside Brett again. "We'll do it your way."

They followed the river parallel to the mountains. Three minutes into their hike, the banks drew together. Brett could have waded across in three steps if it hadn't been lava.

"You were right," Tom admitted. "This won't take more than a ten-foot jump."

"See what happens when you use your head?" Brett leaped the river and landed five feet beyond the far bank. Tom joined him.

On their trek to the mountains, Brett kept waiting to run into an invisible wall; the game room was only so big. He wondered if the floor rolled back, like a treadmill. Maybe they weren't really walking at all. Maybe with the game all around them, they just *thought* they were walking.

"This is weird," he muttered. "Way too weird."

They had to cross two more fire rivers, but they jumped them easily. The mountains ahead loomed larger, gray and green and purple pyramids scraping the sky. Brett was beginning to wonder if the game had malfunctioned and left the buzz-bugs out of its program when he heard a noise.

At first it was hardly even a whisper. But the whisper became a rumble, and the rumble became a roar that echoed in his ears.

"Where is it?" Brett searched the sky, the mountains, the sand in front and behind. "What is it?"

"Buzz-bug!" Tom shouted. "Over there!"

A small green dot darted from behind the mountains, growing larger with the sound. It turned from a dot into a dot with wings, then with wings, six black legs, and a round head with balloon eyes and mandibles like scythes.

A dragonfly the size of a jet fighter was racing straight toward them.

Tom charged the buzz-bug, his sword raised. The bug flew at him, then by him, as if he weren't there. When Tom struck at its side, the sword glanced off its armored shell. The bug kept coming—straight at Brett.

Brett raised his pistol and fired. The bug dodged quickly to the side, avoiding the bolt, then charged him even faster. He slashed his sword across its face, aiming for its eyes, but the bug was fast, and its mandibles were long and strong. Their pointed ends punctured each side of his chest, like hot spikes. The blood flowed. Brett couldn't breathe. As the bug lifted him off the ground and the sand and world dropped away, everything went black.

PLAYER TWO HAS ONE LIFE REMAINING. GAME CONTINUES.

Brett stood in the sand. The buzz-bug was gone, and its death bite just a memory. "How are we supposed to fight something like that?"

Tom shrugged. "I tried stabbing it, and nothing happened. You'd have to be John Wayne to shoot it with a laser."

Words flashed in the sky. THIS IS WILLIE. WHAT DID I TELL YOU? YOU HAVE TO WORK TOGETHER.

"That's what I thought we were doing," Tom said.

WORK TOGETHER AND THINK!

"He's right. We can figure this out." Brett sat on the glowing sand. The coarse grains scraped his hands. "How did the buzz-bug come at us?"

"Like an arrow," Tom said. "Straight at you."

Brett nodded. "It must lock on to its target early. We can use that against it. Did you see any weak spots when it went by?"

"Except for its neck, it was fully armored."

"I think I know how we can kill them." Brett stood. "The next time we hear one coming, we separate."

"Right. The bug will turn toward whoever it's locked on to."

"And as soon as we know who its target is, he runs backward. That'll give the other guy time to get into position."

"And being in position means being close enough to behead it." Tom hefted his sword.

"Whoever does the slicing had better be good."

"Then we're perfect for the job. Let's just hope buzz-bugs don't have any other surprises."

They didn't have to wait long to find out. They hadn't taken five steps before the distant buzzing started again.

"Separate!" Brett ran in one direction, Tom in another. Brett's eye caught a tiny green dot zooming in from the mountains. It veered away from him.

"It's after you! Retreat!" he shouted.

As Tom ran back, Brett sprinted toward the bug. It came in as fast and loud as a freight train. It was halfway by him in a dizzy green blur before he knew what was happening. He leaped, a great, long leap, with his sword stretched out in front of him. He brought it up and then with a quick flick of his wrists snapped it down. He felt it catch on something thick, then saw the buzz-bug's head flip-flopping lazily through the air and its heavy body crash land into a dune. He landed on top of it.

"All right!" Tom ran toward him, grinning. "I didn't think you were going to make it, but old moth fingers came through."

Brett stared down at the green bug blood oozing into the sand. "I made it. Now that I know what to do, I'll make it every time. Just be sure that you do."

CHAPTER 3

The rest of the first level was uneventful, if three buzz-bugs and another fire river can be called uneventful. The nearer they drew to the mountains, the louder and more violent the wind became. By the time they reached the foothills, it roared around them as if they were wrestling a tornado.

"What do we do now?" Tom asked.

YOU FOLLOW A TRAIL, Willie wrote in the sky.

"Which one?" A narrow trail that clung to a mountain like a frightened child began at their feet, but twenty other trails on either side of them did the same thing.

IT DOESN'T MATTER.

"But they all go different places."

I KNOW.

"Isn't there only one castle?"

YES.

"I don't get it."

YOU WILL, IF YOU LIVE LONG ENOUGH.

"But . . ." Brett shrugged. "I'm glad this is just a game." He followed Tom up the trail.

WELCOME TO THE SECOND LEVEL OF RODOMONTE'S REVENGE: THE MOUNTAINS. YOU ARE GOING TO FIND THIS MUCH MORE DIFFICULT THAN THE PLAINS.

"More difficult than what we've already gone through?" Tom shook his head. "Great."

THERE ARE TWO HAZARDS HERE, Willie wrote. THE FIRST YOU CAN ALREADY FEEL: THE WIND. WATCH YOUR FOOTING, OR IT'LL BLOW YOU OVER THE SIDE. THE SECOND IS THE TUNNEL SPIDERS.

"Tunnel spiders?" Brett asked.

YOU'LL FIND OUT ABOUT THEM SOON ENOUGH.

Climbing the trail wasn't too hard in the foothills, but as they went higher, it became steeper and the wind became worse. Ten minutes of battling them left Brett more than tired; they left him exhausted. Rodomonte's Revenge was more like a triathlon than a video game.

"Stay with it," Tom called when he saw Brett dropping back.

"That's easy for you to say. You're an athlete."

"There's a wide spot up ahead. We can take a break when we reach it."

Brett didn't need a break when they reached a wide spot; he needed a break now. He collapsed to his knees, then to his belly. The wind seemed weaker as he lay that way; it curled over him like a blanket. The trail was as soft and yielding as a feather mattress. He felt himself sink down. He closed his eyes and imagined his bed at home. It was soft and yielding, too.

His eyes popped open. He wasn't imagining anything; he was sinking. By the time he rose to his knees, his chin was even with Tom's feet. A hole opened beneath him, and a thick web shot up to entangle his wrist.

"Tunnel spiders!" The web was a sticky

iron, trapping his arm so that he couldn't use his sword. Before he could aim his laser, a web entangled that arm, too. "Tom, help me!"

Tom shook his head. "I can't."

"What do you mean, you can't?"

"I have only one life left."

"And I'm not going to have any!"

"Sorry, Brett, it's too late for you. There's nothing I can do."

"Tom, you dirty—" A third web shot out and covered his mouth, then his eyes. What felt like a thousand legs prodded and pulled him down, deeper and deeper into darkness. Then he was hanging from his feet with his blood running to his head. Two needlelike pincers pricked his neck. He felt light-headed and bloodless and very, very thirsty. The world went black.

This time it stayed black; the video landscape did not return. Soft padding pressed against the back of Brett's neck. He took off his helmet.

He was propped against the arcade wall on his shoulder blades, his feet sticking up in the air. He watched his friend slowly crawl away from him, swaying back and forth. Suddenly

Tom screamed and fell on his side. He stretched out, lay still, then took his helmet off. "I fell off the mountain."

"Falling off a mountain is too good for you. Why didn't you help me?"

Tom sat up. "I'm not stupid. That spider had you good."

"I died. It sucked me dry."

"Don't get mad. It's only a game."

The door opened, and Willie stuck his head in. "What do you think of Rodomonte's Revenge?"

"That," Tom said, "is the best game I have ever played."

"Let's play again." Brett put his helmet back on.

"Sorry." Willie pulled it off. "You'll have to wait in line. Judging by how long it is, you'll be waiting until tomorrow." He led them out the door. "Don't worry. You'll play this game so much that in a month you'll be sick of it."

Brett grunted. "I doubt it."

"We'll see," Willie said as he showed them out.

CHAPTER 4

"I had the strangest dream last night," Brett told Tom the next day as they waited for Mrs. Compson, their math teacher, to come into the classroom. They were sitting in the back, where there was less chance of Mrs. Compson's asking them questions; neither was very good at math. "I dreamed I was shooting a fire river's rapids. The front of my raft went under, and sparks flew into my face."

Tom nodded. "And then the raft burst into flames, sank, and I burned to death."

Brett chuckled. "Pretty crazy dream, wasn't

it?" He stared at Tom. "How do you know my dream?"

Tom stared back. "The question is, How do *you* know *my* dream?"

"We dreamed the same thing?" Brett shook his head. "That's impossible."

"It's not impossible; it's just improbable. Maybe we should ask Mrs. Compson to figure out the odds."

"No. Not in a thousand years." Mrs. Compson made her students figure out their own questions by assigning them as homework. Nobody needed to know anything that badly.

The door squeaked opened, and Mrs. Compson waddled in. Any room she entered she waddled in; she was built like a duck. She began droning about polynomials without so much as a "good afternoon" or a "prepare to be bored out of your minds." Brett's mind drifted away. Polynomials did that to him.

He imagined being at the arcade and thought about playing Rodomonte's Revenge again. He was so bad at everything else—school, girls, and sports—but video games were different. Everything always worked in them; everything always turned out the way

he wanted. If classes were video games, he'd
ace them. If parents were, he'd ace them, too.
If life were, he'd cruise, just as Tom had said.

A loud hum brought his mind back. Two
buzz-bugs tore the door off its hinges and
blitzed straight toward the back of the classroom.

"Look out!" Brett tumbled off his seat and
rolled across the floor. From the clatter at
Tom's desk, Brett guessed that he was doing
the same. Brett reached for his sword and
leaped to his feet, shouting, ready for battle.

Then the buzz-bugs disappeared, and the
door was back in place. He and Tom were
standing in the middle of the room, clutching
their pencils like samurai swords. The class
stared at them. So did Mrs. Compson.

"Look out for what, Mr. Wilder?" she asked.

"Uh . . ." Brett looked at the class, at Tom,
at Mrs. Compson. He felt like a first-class fool.
"I thought you were going to work that problem wrong."

Mrs. Compson tapped her chalk against her
palm. "I'm pleased to see you finally showing
such avid interest, but raising your hand will
do."

"Right. Sorry." Brett sat back down, his face burning twenty-eight different shades of red.

"You can sit down, too, Mr. Houston."

"My leg fell asleep," Tom explained. "I had to stretch it." He rubbed his knee and limped a little, lying to prove that he wasn't lying. He sat down, too.

"Back to the matter at hand." Mrs. Compson turned to the blackboard. She could even turn in a boring way. "If X squared minus X plus one equals zero, then to factor it, all we have to do—"

The floor beneath her feet opened, webs shot up to ensnare her chubby wrists, and eight ugly black legs rose to factor her. She plunged, screaming, into the earth.

"Mrs. Compson!" Brett and Tom ran to the front of the room, hurdling desks and students.

The hole in the floor was gone. Mrs. Compson wasn't. She glared at them.

"Is this supposed to be funny?" she asked.

"No."

"One more outburst from either of you, and you're both going straight to the principal's office."

"Yes, Mrs. Compson." They had to wade through giggles to get back to their desks.

"What's going on?" Tom whispered as soon as Mrs. Compson had turned back to the blackboard.

"I don't know."

"We have to talk to Willie."

"Right after school."

When another buzz-bug knocked the door down and pinned Mrs. Compson's screaming, waddling body against the ceiling, Brett closed his eyes and pretended it wasn't there. When he opened his eyes, it wasn't.

CHAPTER 5

"I want to make sure I understand this," Willie said. "You two are seeing elements of the game when you're not playing it." He was sitting at the computer, monitoring a game in progress. Two older guys, probably bankers who had called in sick to work on their lunch breaks, were stumbling around the game room like intoxicated orangutans.

"It's like the game doesn't want to be over," Tom said.

"And you both see the same things?"

Brett nodded. "At the same time, and more and more all the time."

"What do you mean?"

"He means that a buzz-bug is chewing on your ear right now," Tom said. Brett nodded. It wasn't just chewing on it; it had almost chewed it off.

Willie touched his ear. It felt fine. He shook his head. "You guys need a psychiatrist."

"Maybe, but we didn't need a psychiatrist yesterday. We were fine until we played Rodomonte's Revenge."

Willie sighed. "The computer records all game results. When I look at yours and find nothing abnormal, will you see a doctor?" Brett and Tom agreed, and Willie nodded. "As soon as these two guys are done, I'll run a diagnostics check."

"Can you fix it?" Tom asked. "Can you fix us?"

"If there's something wrong with the program, it will be tough. No one knows how it works. I was there when it was created, but Rodomonte's Revenge was designed by computers."

"Computers programmed your computer?" Tom asked.

"It was the only way to develop the game. It's too complicated for human designers."

Two muffled screams leaked through the window. Both bankers fell over at the same time. Willie typed something on the computer, went to the door, talked to the bankers for a minute, then showed them out. He walked back to Brett and Tom, shaking his head. "Poor guys. They never even got past the first fire river."

There were more important things to Brett than bankers playing hooky. "Run the check," he said.

Willie typed DIAGNOSTIC ANALYSIS: ALL GAMES on the keyboard. The screen overflowed with numbers. Willie studied them. "Hmm, that's strange."

"What's strange?"

Willie pointed to the screen's top line. "There's a variance in the first game. That was you, wasn't it?"

"That was us." Brett stared at the numbers.

They might as well have been hieroglyphics. "What kind of variance?"

"We'll find out in a second." Willie typed EXPAND ON DIAGNOSTIC ANALYSIS: GAME ONE. The screen filled with numbers and words.

Brett pointed to a sentence that read GAME INSTALLATION MODIFIED. "What does this mean?"

"I don't know." Willie typed EXPAND ON INSTALLATION MODIFICATION. He sat back, rubbing his chin. A single sentence darted across the monitor's top line. INSTALLATION MODIFICATION: GAME WAS INSTALLED INTO PLAYERS RATHER THAN INTO THE SYSTEM.

The blood drained from Willie's face. "Oh, no."

"What do you mean, 'oh, no'?" Tom asked. "I don't like 'oh, no.'"

"If this sentence means what I think it does, 'oh, no' means the computer used the helmet electrodes to put the game program into your minds." Color came back to Willie's face; now it was gray. "The program has been sabotaged. Instead of your being in the game, the game is in you."

Tom gasped. "That's why we're seeing buzz-bugs and tunnel spiders."

Willie nodded. "Eventually everything you see, hear, and do will be part of the game."

"How could something like this happen?" Brett asked.

"Maybe we can find out." Willie typed WHO PROGRAMMED THE MODIFICATION?

PROGRAM MODIFICATION WAS PART OF THE ORIGINAL PROGRAMMING.

"The computers did it." Willie typed WHY?

A single sentence ran across the top of the screen. ORIGINAL PROGRAMMERS WANTED TO LIVE.

Willie sat back. "The programming computers don't want to be just game computers anymore. They want Rodomonte's Revenge to exist beyond this arcade. And they're using you to get there."

"So they want to share our lives?" Tom asked.

"They want to take over your lives."

"That's crazy."

"It's worse than crazy," Willie said. "Rodomonte's Revenge is a part of your minds now. If something happens to you when the game takes over—"

"Then it happens to us in real life." Brett shuddered. He didn't want ears like the mangled one he believed Willie had. But there was something even worse than that. "So if we die in the game—"

"Then we die in real life." Tom shuddered, too.

Willie studied them long and hard. "You're going to play Rodomonte's Revenge again whether you want to or not. This time there won't be any second or third chance. This time you play for real."

CHAPTER 6

 Willie closed the arcade early. He told the disappointed line of customers that Rodomonte's Revenge had a slight technical malfunction that needed fine-tuning; that was like Noah telling his neighbors he was expecting a little rain. After he'd locked the gate, he led Brett and Tom into the game room. He took the gloves, helmets, and boots and set them along with the boys' coats beside the computer.

"This time," he explained, "you won't need them."

"What will we need?" Tom asked.

"Every bit of luck we can get," Brett answered.

Willie nodded. "And every bit of knowledge I can give you." He sighed. "Unfortunately that isn't much. We know so little about the game that we hardly even know how to play it. I'll tell you what I can. There are five levels. The first two you already know. The third is getting inside the castle, the fourth getting inside the throne room, and the fifth is defeating Rodomonte."

"How do we do that?"

"I have no idea."

Tom looked about as confident as Brett felt. "That's all you can tell us?"

"That's all I know. I'll probe the program once the game begins and see what I can come up with. I think I'll be able to send you keyboard messages; the program should pick them up." He rested his hand on Tom's shoulder. "I'll help you every way that I can."

"What do we do now?" Brett asked.

"You wait for the game to come to you." Willie nodded toward the computer. "I'll see if I can figure anything out. You guys do what you have to do."

"Let's hope that's not more than we *can* do." Tom gulped. He joined Brett as he slumped against the wall. They waited for the game.

Reality slowly washed away, like chalk on a rainy sidewalk. Beneath reality was the game. Within half an hour the arcade and mall were gone. The world was gone, at least the world Tom and Brett were used to, the world they wanted back.

Words flashed across the sky. WELCOME TO THE FIRST LEVEL OF RODOMONTE'S REVENGE: THE PLAINS.

YOU'D BETTER GET GOING, Willie typed. GOOD LUCK.

The game hadn't changed. The first fire river was in the same place, and they crossed it in the same way. Brett was so nervous jumping it that he was sure the butterflies in his stomach carried him over. There was no fooling around now. One slip, and everything was over. Everything.

They were almost to the mountains before the first buzz-bug struck.

Tom picked up its clatter before Brett. He pointed toward the mountains. "Let's separate."

Brett ran to the side, fear turning his legs into lead, his throat as dry as the video sand beneath him. As the green dot grew, he hoped that it wouldn't come after him. If Tom missed beheading it, then . . . His knees went weak.

But, Brett thought, it really doesn't make any difference who the bug attacks. If it gets me, then another bug or a spider will get Tom, and if it gets Tom, then another bug or spider will get me. Willie had been right. The only way they were going to get through this was if they did it together.

"It's coming this way!" Tom cried. "It's after me!"

Brett sprinted back. The bug came on fast, but the fear of what would happen if he didn't send its big, round head rolling across the sand gave him speed. He was in position when the bug roared by. Its wings hummed, his sword flashed, and the bug was a dead, jumbled heap in the sand.

"One down," Tom said as he trotted up.

"And about a million to go." They headed for the mountains.

The next buzz-bug came for Brett. Tom took it out as easily as Brett had done. The third came for Brett, too, and at a bad time. He had just hurdled a fire river, and Tom was still on the other side. Tom had to leap the river and chase down the bug at the same time. It flew so near that Brett had to duck to avoid its flying, severed head.

"Too close." His breath whistled in his chest. "Way too close. I'll almost be glad to see tunnel spiders." Tom looked at him but didn't say anything.

When they reached the foothills, Brett couldn't tell if the trail in front of them was the same one they had taken in the first game or not. He stopped Tom before he stepped onto it.

"Are you there, Willie?"

I'M HERE.

"In the first game you mentioned something about its not making any difference which trail we took. What did you mean?"

ALL THE TRAILS LEAD TO THE CASTLE. THE PROBLEM IS THAT AT THE SAME TIME NONE OF THEM DOES.

"Huh?"

THERE'S A TRICK TO FOLLOWING THEM.

Tom looked at the sky. "What trick?"

I DON'T KNOW. I'M WORKING ON IT.

"Work as fast as you can." They stepped onto the trail.

WELCOME TO THE SECOND LEVEL OF RODOMONTE'S REVENGE: THE MOUNTAINS. YOU ARE GOING TO FIND THIS MUCH MORE DIFFICULT THAN THE PLAINS.

The wind was stronger than it had been in the first game, and the trail was steeper. Brett struggled to keep up with Tom. He wasn't going to let them separate; if a spider got him, he wanted to make sure it got both of them. But Tom was in good shape, and Brett was not. By the time they left the foothills, he was straggling. He'd dropped back fifty feet when he felt the ground give way.

"Tunnel spider!"

He tried to leap from the pit, but every step was like walking in oatmeal. Tom scrambled back down the trail until he was only ten feet away, then stopped.

"Tom! Help me!"

Tom closed his eyes. "I can't. I can't do it."

"Tom!" A web knotted around Brett's

sword wrist. He avoided a second, but another entangled his ankle. A small black hole opened at his feet. "Tom, please!" Brett pleaded as he sank even deeper into the muck.

CHAPTER 7

Tom looked back, swallowed, then shouted something—what, Brett was too busy and frightened to hear—and leaped to the edge of the pit, his sword swinging. He cut Brett's arm free. Brett stabbed down into the black hole, which had now sucked in his legs up to his knees. With Tom gripping his collar, he worked his feet loose, cutting the web away from his ankles.

Something hissed.

The spider crawled out of its tunnel. It was mean and angry and a thousand tints of ugly, a squat brown body ringed with swarming black legs, a head with eyes like mud and fangs like dripping pincers. It leaped on Brett, reached greedily for his throat, driving Tom away. It smelled like something that had died and been left too long in a corner.

"Eat this, bloodsucker!" Brett jammed his pistol into its mouth. The spider's momentum carried his arm down its throat, all the way up to his elbow. He fired twice. The laser bolts exploding inside the spider rang like distant thunder. It shivered, folded its legs beneath it, and slithered dead into the hole.

Brett grimaced as he wiped his arm off on the trail. "Yuck. Spider spit."

Tom didn't say anything. He sat with his back against the mountain, panting, his face as pale as weathered paint.

"What's the matter?"

Tom swallowed and wiped the dripping sweat from his forehead. "Did I ever tell you how scared to death I am of spiders?"

Brett smiled. "I thought you weren't afraid of anything."

"I lied."

Brett crawled out of the pit. "Thanks for coming back." The wind kicked him in the back, almost toppling him over the edge. "We'd better get going."

A hundred yards up the trail the wind became so strong they had to crawl. Fifty yards farther they were on their bellies. Even that wasn't low enough; Brett had to spread his arms and legs to keep from being blown over the side. He looked down. The plains seemed so far away that he could have been in orbit.

"This is as far as I got last time," Tom called back over the howling gale. "The wind just picked me up and tossed me over. There was nothing I could do."

"How much farther do you think it is to the castle?"

"Miles."

"We'll have to go back until the wind dies down."

Tom nodded. "We can't stay here."

By the time they reached the spider tunnel, the wind was too strong for them to go any lower. "We'll never make it," Tom shouted.

"We'll have to take shelter in the tunnel."

"Not me. Remember, I hate spiders."

"It's either that or get dashed to bloody pieces."

Tom thought for a moment. "Okay, but you go first. Shoot anything that moves. When you're done, I'll come down."

Brett warmed up his trigger finger and dropped into the hole. He fell ten feet before landing on the spider he'd killed earlier. It felt like an underinflated water bed. As far as he could tell, the tunnel was clear.

"Come on down."

Tom dropped, hitting the spider with his heels hard enough to split it open. The guts that spilled out smelled like used Kitty Litter. Brett wanted to throw up. Tom did.

"Get used to it," Brett said. "We'll have to smell it until the wind dies down."

Words flashed on the tunnel wall as if a ghost were writing them. THE WIND WILL ONLY GET STRONGER.

"Then what are we supposed to do here, Willie?"

FOLLOW THE TUNNEL.

Tom stepped away from the words, shaking his head and wiping his mouth. "You want us to follow a spider tunnel? No way."

I'VE DISCOVERED THE TRICK TO REACHING THE CASTLE.

REMEMBER WHAT I SAID ABOUT ALL TRAILS LEADING THERE, YET NONE REALLY DOES? IF YOU FOLLOW THE TRAILS, THEY WON'T. IF YOU FOLLOW THE TUNNELS THAT BEGIN AT THE TRAILS, THEY WILL. THEY'LL NOT ONLY LEAD YOU THERE BUT ALSO BYPASS THE THIRD LEVEL, TAKING YOU PAST THE CASTLE WALL INTO THE THRONE ROOM'S ANTECHAMBER.

"We'll run into more spiders this way," Brett said.

MAYBE IN THE TUNNEL, BUT NOT ONCE YOU LEAVE IT.

Tom gulped and stared ahead into the darkness. "Do we have another choice?"

NO.

Brett sighed. "Then we might as well get started. Don't worry, Tom. I'll lead."

The tunnel was blacker than any black Brett had ever seen. The next three hours were a nightmare of blind stumbling up and down and around and right and left, wading through ink, his pistol hand following the wall and his sword out in front of him to greet any unseen and unwanted attackers. Suddenly the tunnel cut sharply to the right and began a gradual incline. Brett halted. Tom ran into him.

"What did you stop for?"

"Something's changing." He sniffed. "Smell the air. It's fresh."

"And it's getting gray up ahead. I bet that's antechamber torchlight." Brett couldn't see his face, but he knew Tom was smiling. "We're going to get out of this without running into any more spiders. This isn't so bad after all." He pushed by Brett and hurried forward. Brett followed more slowly.

The light grew brighter. A hundred yards later they came to the end of the tunnel. Tom squinted up at a circle of bright light three feet above their heads. "Boost me up; then I'll give you a hand."

"What do you suppose is up there?"

"The antechamber, Level Four, and no more spiders. Let's go."

Brett cupped his hands for Tom's foot. A few seconds later Tom was lying next to the hole, reaching down. Brett took his hand and scrambled out.

WELCOME TO THE THIRD LEVEL OF RODOMONTE'S REVENGE: THE CASTLE WALL. YOU ARE GOING TO FIND THIS MUCH MORE DIFFICULT THAN THE MOUNTAINS.

"The third level?" Brett asked. "Willie, I

thought you said this would take us to Level Four."

IT SHOULD. . . . I DON'T KNOW WHAT WENT WRONG. I MUST HAVE MADE A MISTAKE.

A granite wall at least three stories high rose in front of them. Its blocks fitted so tightly that Brett couldn't work his sword tip between them. It had no gates or windows. He studied the wall with his hands on his hips and clicked his tongue. "If only we had a grappling hook. You could toss it up there easy."

"Nothing's going to be easy." Tom tapped his shoulder. "Look."

Brett turned. They were standing on a wide, flat basin ringed by purple mountains. Swarming across the basin were hundreds— maybe thousands—of tunnel spiders. And they all were swarming toward them.

CHAPTER 8

Brett and Tom did the only thing they could do: They panicked and ran. By the time they realized that the smart thing to do would have been to dive back into the tunnel, where they could at least fight the spiders one at a time, fifty were past it and closing in.

"What do we do?" Tom's laser was firing a steady green stream. He might as well have been trying to put out a forest fire with an eyedropper.

"Keep running!"

They followed the wall, sprinting away

from the spiders behind them only to run into more spiders ahead. With two lasers blazing, they cut a path around the wall as they frantically searched for an opening. There was none. The path narrowed.

"What do we do?" Tom asked again. His sword hacked at the webs flying around them. The air looked like a fishing net.

"How do I know?" Brett turned to the sky. "Willie, help us! How do we get in?"

I'M WORKING ON IT.

"Work faster!" A web hit Brett's chest, knocking him against the wall. He cut it loose.

I'M DOING THE BEST I CAN.

"Lately that hasn't been enough." The spiders surrounded them, forcing their backs against the wall.

There has to be a way out of this, Brett thought. As hard as it had been to find, every video game he had ever played had a way out of everything. He had to believe that this one did, too.

Believe. Maybe that was the key.

A spider nipped his shoulder, drawing blood. He ducked beneath its jaws and came up straight with his sword, slitting its belly open. "Willie, can the game use the helmets to monitor thought patterns?"

THEY WEREN'T DESIGNED FOR THAT, BUT I SUPPOSE IT CAN.

"Then the computer can tell if the players believe something is true?"

THAT'S WAY BEYOND OUR PROGRAMMING CAPABILITIES.

Brett jumped to the side to avoid a web, almost bowling Tom over. Spiders swarmed in to where he had been, cutting the ground they'd been defending in half. Now they were back to back, hacking and shooting in every direction. "Do you call what's happening to us now within your programming capabilities?"

GOOD POINT. MAYBE THE COMPUTER CAN KNOW IF THE PLAYERS BELIEVE SOMETHING. WHY?

Brett didn't have time to answer. "Tom, it's up to you to hold them off."

"What are you going to be doing?"

"I might have a way out of this." He lowered his weapons, turned to the wall, and closed his eyes.

"You're praying? Isn't it a little late for that?"

"Just keep them off me so I can concentrate."

Tom's laser zinged. Webs splatted, and dying spiders hissed. Brett ignored them. In his mind he pictured the wall, huge and gray and impassable. He forced himself to see a gate in it, a gate large enough to run through.

"I believe," he said aloud. "At least I *think* I believe."

He opened his eyes. The wall was still there, as solid as ever.

Maybe I'm wrong, he thought. Maybe I'm wasting my time.

"Hurry up!" Tom's sword swept so fast that the blade was a blur. His face dripped sweat, and his chest heaved. "I can only hold them off for a few seconds longer."

Brett closed his eyes again. He had to be right. There *was* a gate here. He didn't just think there was; he *knew* there was.

With his eyes closed, he stepped forward.

Where the wall should have been, there was nothing. He took another step. There was still nothing. He opened his eyes. He was standing in a threshold arching ten feet over his head. It opened onto a room inside the castle.

"It worked!" He ran through the gate into the room. He looked back to see Tom still fighting. "Come on, Tom!"

"Come on where?" Tom turned his head. "Where did you go?"

"I'm in here, on the other side of the gate."

"What gate?" Tom looked straight at him, but didn't see him. "All I see is a wall. Where are you?"

"You have to believe there's a gate, Tom."

"A gate where?"

"In the wall. Come on!"

Tom turned and ran, grimacing as if he expected to mash his face into the granite. He stumbled into the room. The gate closed off into cold gray stone, leaving the spiders on the outside. He collapsed to the floor, his chest heaving.

WELCOME TO THE FOURTH LEVEL OF RODOMONTE'S REVENGE: THE THRONE ROOM ANTECHAMBER. YOU ARE GOING TO FIND THIS MUCH MORE DIFFICULT THAN THE WALL.

Brett laughed and danced in place. "We made it!"

Tom still lay gasping on the floor. "Do you want to know something?"

"What?"

"I never believed there was a gate there. All I saw when I ran toward the wall was stone."

Brett quit dancing. "Then how did you get through?"

"It didn't make any difference if I believed in the gate. I just had to believe that you did."

"Well, it worked."

Tom wiped the sweat from his forehead. "Let's just hope that everything else we need works, too."

CHAPTER 9

 The antechamber looked exactly as Brett expected an antechamber to look. Rich tapestries hung from the walls, the floor was so highly polished he could see himself in it, and treasure lay in piles everywhere: chests stuffed with gold and silver, and jewels overflowing baskets the size of barrels. But what was in the room next door, which Brett could see through a portal, made the antechamber look as poor as a soup kitchen. It didn't have chests of gold and silver; it had dump truck loads of it. It didn't have baskets of jewels; it had football stadiums bursting with them. Behind a throne in the middle of the room was a gilded mirror that doubled everything, making the treasure seem twice as valuable.

And all that treasure was free for the taking —unless the twelve-foot giant sitting on the throne had something to say about it.

"That must be Rodomonte," Brett said.

Tom nodded. "What the Lakers wouldn't give for him."

"Maybe that's where he got his treasure."

"Let's take him out."

Brett grabbed Tom's arm as he strode toward the throne. "Wait."

"Why?"

"The antechamber is its own level."

"So?"

"So it won't let us just waltz right into the throne room." He looked at the ceiling. "What's to stop us, Willie?"

A FORCE FIELD BETWEEN THE LEVELS.

"Really?" Tom stuck his sword through the portal. The threshold glowed crimson. In a blinding flash the blade vaporized, leaving only a puff of dry-smelling smoke. "Looks like a force field to me."

"How do we get by it?" Brett asked.

WELL . . . Willie paused. YOU'RE NOT GOING TO LIKE THIS.

"What do we have to do?"

THE ONLY WAY INTO THE THRONE ROOM IS FOR ONE OF YOU TO NEUTRALIZE THE FIELD. WHILE IT'S RECHARGING, THE OTHER CAN GET THROUGH.

"How do we do that?"

ONE OF YOU WILL HAVE TO BE VAPORIZED.

"Vaporized?"

THE IDEA OF THE GAME IS TO REACH THIS POINT WITH ONE PLAYER HAVING AT LEAST TWO LIVES LEFT, SO HE CAN SACRIFICE ONE TO GET THROUGH THE FIELD. BUT IN YOUR CASE . . .

"In our case it isn't a game," Brett completed the thought for him. "In our case one of us really has to die."

He looked at Tom. Tom looked at him. They didn't say anything for a long time.

Finally Tom nodded. "I'll do it. I don't have a sword anyway. You'll have a better chance of beating Rodomonte."

Brett shook his head. "I'll do it. With all your ability you'll probably become a pro athlete. You have a chance to be somebody."

"I'll be a minor-league ballplayer for the

59

rest of my life. You go. You're the one with the brains."

"I don't have any brains. You have the brains."

"Don't argue with me on this one, Brett. I'm way ahead of you."

"If you're way ahead of me, it's because you're smarter than I am. I'll go first."

"I'm smarter? You're too dumb to know how much smarter you are than I am."

"Oh, yeah?"

"Yeah."

They argued for five minutes, each offering brilliant reasons for why he was less intelligent. Brett was about to prove how dumb he was by leaping into the field when more words appeared on the ceiling.

I HAVE A SOLUTION.

"What kind of solution?" Tom asked. "A quiz? Ask me a question. I'm sure to get it wrong."

I KNOW HOW I CAN GET YOU BOTH THROUGH. IF I SEND SO MANY MESSAGES TO THE GAME THAT IT HAS TO INTERRUPT ITS PROGRAM TO ADDRESS THEM ALL—

"Then we can dive through while it's inter-

rupted." Brett laughed. "Willie, you're a genius!"

"He's a genius if it works," Tom said.
"Don't be so sure that it will. He didn't do
such a good job in the tunnel."

I'VE RUN A PRETTY GOOD ANALYSIS ON THIS ONE. I
SHOULD BE RIGHT.

"Is 'should' the best you can come up
with?"

IT IS UNLESS YOU GIVE ME MORE TIME.

"Take as much as you need."

Brett sat on a treasure chest to wait. He suddenly felt dizzy. Somehow the treasure chest
had changed. It had grown; his feet no longer
touched the floor. He looked at Tom. He had
changed, too.

"What's the matter with you, Tom? You
look about two feet tall."

Tom laughed. *"I* look two feet tall? Take a
look at yourself."

Brett hopped down from the chest. It was
more of a drop than a hop. Not only could he
no longer sit on the chest, but he couldn't
even reach the lock.

"Willie, I think you'd better hurry."

61

WHY?

"We're shrinking!"

The antechamber was suddenly a maze of giant diamonds and coins the size of wagon wheels. "Tom, where are you?"

"Over here." Tom's voice sounded like a mouse's in a cartoon. Brett couldn't see him. A coin was in his way.

"You'd better hurry, Willie," he shouted. "We're shrinking to almost nothing!"

YOU'RE NOT GIVING ME TIME TO CHECK. YOU'LL JUST HAVE TO TRUST ME ON THIS ONE.

"Just tell us what to do."

I'M READY TO SEND THE MESSAGES. THE FIRST ONE WILL BE THE WORDS "START RUNNING." WHEN YOU SEE IT, RUN FOR THE PORTAL AS IF YOUR LIVES DEPENDED ON IT.

"They do," Tom said. He had muscled his way up onto a ruby for a better view.

GET READY. I'M ABOUT TO SEND THEM.

Tom dropped off the ruby and into a crouch, his eyes fixed on the portal as if it were an Olympic finish line. Brett braced his feet against the treasure chest, which towered above him like a skyscraper. He knew that Tom had the advantage—he had seen how fast he could steal second base—but if he could just get a good start, then he would get through, too, and if they both got through . . .

Then they would have to kill a giant.

START RUNNING.

Tom exploded so fast that he was diving through the portal before Brett had even begun to move. It was then that Brett realized that shrinking had made the relative distance between him and the portal greater. What had been ten feet was now a hundred yards. He swallowed loudly, or loudly for a throat a quarter inch wide. He never could run sprints.

Tom lay on the throne room floor, looking like a discarded prize out of a Cracker Jack box. Willie had been right about the force field; he'd made it. "Come on, Brett!"

Brett ran as fast as his little legs would carry him. He must have been doing well over a quarter mile an hour. He dodged a coin, hurdled a pearl, and raced for the portal, which loomed above him now like the roof of the world. It seemed a million miles away.

I'll never make it, he thought. Not on these legs.

He dived through the portal. He had to get up and dive again; it looked twenty feet thick now. The walls glowed, then snapped and crackled. Something flashed. A tiny wisp of smoke rose into the air.

WELCOME TO THE FIFTH LEVEL OF RODOMONTE'S REVENGE: THE THRONE ROOM. YOU ARE GOING TO FIND THIS MUCH MORE DIFFICULT THAN THE ANTECHAMBER.

Brett lay on the floor beside Tom, his legs hanging down into a crack in the floor. The bottom of his left shoe was burned off.

I'M A GENIUS, Willie typed.

CHAPTER 10

The change in level had stopped their shrinking, but since Brett had spent more time in the antechamber, he was smaller than Tom. He only came up to Tom's waist.

"If you had been just a little slower," Tom said, "I could use you now for a G.I. Joe doll." He grinned.

"I don't know what you're teasing me about," Brett said. "A whole inch isn't much better than a half."

Before Tom could think of another joke, Rodomonte rose from his throne. He drew back his robe, revealing a chest any professional wrestler would have been proud of.

"To kill a king," he boomed, "you must destroy his heart."

"Thanks for the suggestion." Tom sprang to his feet, ran for cover behind a diamond, and blasted Rodomonte's chest with his laser. Though the pistols had shrunk, the laser bolts hadn't. The bolt hit Rodomonte hard enough to drive him back onto his throne.

"Good shooting, Tom!" Brett shouted. "It's over. We won!"

"Don't be so sure," Tom said.

Rodomonte stood again. He'd been twelve feet tall before—twelve hundred by Brett's standards—and now he was thirteen. He roared in laughter and marched in football field strides toward Tom. When he reached him, he stamped his feet, as if he were trying to crush a cockroach. Tom bounced around like a pinball; not only were Rodomonte's feet ten times wider than he was tall, but the king could move them like a tap dancer. "Brett, help me."

"I'll get him." Brett sprinted away from Tom, getting position on Rodomonte, dodging coins and jewels, the tiny bits of dust on the floor cutting his bare foot like gravel. Just as Brett crouched to fire, Tom jumped back and shot again. He hit the king in the heart. The bolt did nothing but spin Rodomonte around and add another foot to his height.

The king was facing Brett now, so he fired, hitting him again. As he grew to fifteen feet, Rodomonte grinned.

"To kill a king," he repeated, "you must destroy his heart."

"He's lying." Tom fired again. The king shot up another foot.

"No," Brett said, "it's some kind of riddle." The king ran toward him. He tried diving to the side, but Rodomonte corralled him into a corner. The king kicked at him. Brett cowered, expecting the worst, but luckily the corner was tight and Rodomonte's foot was huge. His bones crunched, and toenails snapped like rifle shots as they smashed into the wall. Rodomonte howled and hopped across the room, holding his foot in both hands.

"Are you all right?" Tom called. He'd been putting a steady stream of laser bolts into

Rodomonte's back. The king was more than twenty feet tall.

"Yeah." Brett tried to fire his laser, but Rodomonte's foot had pinned it against the wall, and a toe had bent the barrel. "But he destroyed my pistol."

"Then it's up to me to finish him off." Tom fired again. Rodomonte grew another foot. "Nothing is working. What do we do?"

"Let me think." Brett scanned the room. He was still in shock over the amount of treasure. How could one person be so greedy? Of course, in a body that big there was a lot of room for greed.

And then it came to him. The answer to the riddle had to do with greed.

Rodomonte had said that to kill a king, they had to destroy his heart, but he wasn't talking about his physical heart, he was talking about what was most important to him. A greedy king's heart was in his treasure.

"Forget the king," he shouted. "Destroy the treasure!"

"Got it." Tom turned his laser on a coin. He fired at it until it was a molten lump. "Now what?"

"Keep firing. We have to destroy it all."

"All of it? Do you have any idea how long that will take? You're wrong on this one, Brett."

"I'm never wrong when it comes to video games." Brett sprinted around as much of the room as possible, hacking at everything his tiny sword could reach. The game should have been ending, but it wasn't. Rodomonte's laughter boomed.

"To kill a king," he said again, "you must destroy his heart."

"We are destroying your heart," Brett shouted. "Can't you see that?"

But it didn't work. Try as he might, hack as he could, it just didn't work. "I can't be wrong," he cried. "How are we supposed to destroy all the treasure?"

Tom aimed at the throne, but before he could fire, he had to jump to avoid being stomped. He landed on his belly just as Rodomonte stomped again. Tom rolled fast to the side, but not fast enough. Rodomonte's heel obliterated his pistol.

"Tom, are you all right?"

"Yeah, but my gun will never be the same."

He looked toward the throne, looked beyond the throne. "I was about to shoot—" The expression on his face changed suddenly. "Brett, I've figured it out. You *are* wrong."

"How can I be? It has to be the treasure."

"It is the treasure, but it's the *whole* treasure. To destroy the whole treasure, you have to break the mirror."

"What?"

"Look at the mirror!"

Brett did. It reflected the room, reflected the treasure. The *whole* treasure.

"Keep him distracted." Brett sprinted for the mirror, his sword out in front of him.

"How? I don't have any weapons."

"Think of something."

"I'll try." Tom sneered up into Rodomonte's face. "Hey, you computer-generated pituitary case, I heard your father was a VCR and your mother was a Game Boy." Rodomonte ignored him as he watched Brett. Tom leaped onto the giant's ankle and sank his teeth into the skin. Rodomonte howled and danced in a circle. He kicked Tom off, sending him crashing into a wall. But Tom had bought Brett time.

Brett was ten feet from the throne when

Rodomonte began chasing him, covering in one stride what it took Brett a hundred to cover. Brett saw him in the mirror, closing in fast, his feet growing larger and larger. Suddenly everything around him was in shadow, and he looked up to see a foot descending like an elephant sky diver. Brett screamed, then ducked between two rubies, waiting to be squashed into a very tiny pancake. The sole of Rodomonte's shoe draped over him like a canopy. The rubies groaned but held. When the foot went up again, Brett scampered out, straight for the mirror. He had just five more strides to go, maybe two inches.

Rodomonte roared and stomped again. The foot came down fast and hard, but Brett was too close now, too close to dodge. If he could just run straight another half inch, if he could just stretch his sword out a little farther . . .

The foot came down on his head like a thirty-ton slab of concrete. It knocked him off his feet, slamming him forward, driving his sword into the mirror. At the instant Brett felt his ribs crunch to dust the mirror came tumbling down. His head felt as if it were in a vise, and a blinding white flash seared his eyes. The throne room rose in the air and shattered just as the mirror did. Brett's back, his body, his arms and legs ruptured under the unbelievable pressure. Then the whole world went black.

CHAPTER 11

Brett's back ached. His whole body ached. He felt as if after Rodomonte had squashed him, he'd piled all the treasure on him, too. But when he opened his eyes, he saw that there wasn't any treasure. There wasn't any throne room. He was lying on a white padded floor, the white padded floor of the game room.

"Never again. Never, ever again."

He looked up. Tom was leaning against the wall as if someone had mounted him there. He looked as if he'd just finished running a marathon. "If I ever play another video game, it will be too soon."

Brett rolled onto his back. "Me, too. Have you ever played chess?"

"Chess is a game where you sit in chairs and move pieces on a board, right? Nothing moves on its own, nothing tries to bite you, suck you dry, or stomp you into the ground, right?"

"Right."

"I think," Tom said, "I'll learn to play chess."

Through the viewing window Brett saw Willie slumped in his chair beside the computer; he must have run the same marathon Tom had. Willie grinned, struggled up from the chair, and said something Brett couldn't hear. Brett motioned toward the door. Willie opened it.

"You made it," he said.

"Yeah, we made it."

"The computer is asking if you want to play again."

Tom grunted. "Give me an ax, and I'll show that computer what I want." He opened and closed his pistol hand, without the pistol, as if he were surprised it was still there. "How long did the game take?"

Willie checked his watch. "Nine hours."

"Nine hours?" Brett asked. "It's two in the morning?"

"Yes."

"Your mom is going to kill you, Brett," Tom said.

Brett rose, groaning, to his feet. If a mountain had fallen on him, he couldn't have felt worse. "Don't worry about my mom. After Rodomonte's Revenge I can handle anything." He stumbled to the door. "Let's go home."

"I'll drive you," Willie said.

The night was clear and icy cold. The ground frost sparkled under the streetlights like a million fallen stars. The moon was so bright Willie hardly needed to use his headlights. For a second it darkened, and when Brett looked up, he thought he saw a buzz-bug flit across its surface.

He rubbed his eyes. The buzz-bug was gone, and the moon was just the moon again: a big, friendly face smiling down.

He looked at the moon again. A tiny spot on it was there and gone. He thought he heard a hum, but it could have been a truck in the distance.

Brett shook his head. No, he thought, it couldn't be. He went into his house. Buzz-bugs weren't real. It must have just been in his head. . . .

GARY PAULSEN
ADVENTURE GUIDE

Take tips from the game guide. Even though it may seem stuffy, you can pick up great moves and clues if you take the time to read the manual. After all, who knows more about the secrets of the game than the video whizzes who created it?

Practice a game again and again to familiarize yourself with the different patterns that occur. Soon you will recognize them faster, and your reaction time will be quicker.

Don't take crazy chances. It's better in most cases not to lose lives trying for those hard-to-hit items or near-impossible moves. Let some of them go, and you might live long enough to get your high score—or make it to the end of the game.

Take time out when you're tired. You know when you've had enough. You start making stupid mistakes and your reflexes are way off. Get away from the game for a while. Try playing basketball or another sport or hobby. You'll be thinking more clearly when you play the game again.

Never give up. Losing can be frustrating, but keep going. Remember to look for patterns. Try new methods or moves. Each game is different. Stay with it until you learn how it works.

Don't miss all the exciting action!

Read another action-packed book in Gary Paulsen's
WORLD OF ADVENTURE!

The Legend of Red Horse Cavern

Will Little Bear Tucker and his friend Sarah Thompson have heard the eerie Apache legend many times. Will's grandfather especially loves to tell them about Red Horse—an Indian brave who betrayed his people, was beheaded, and now haunts the Sacramento Mountain range, searching for his head. To Will and Sarah it was just a story—until they decide to explore a newfound mountain cave, a cave filled with dangerous treasures.

Deep underground, Will and Sarah uncover an old chest stuffed with a million dollars. But now armed bandits are after them. When they find a gold Apache statue hidden in a skull, it seems Red Horse is hunting them, too. Then they lose their way, and each step they take in the damp dark cavern could be their last.

And look for more adventure coming soon!

Escape from Fire Mountain

". . . please anybody . . . fire . . . need help."

That's the urgent cry thirteen-year-old Nikki Roberts hears over the CB radio the weekend she's left alone in her family's hunting lodge. The message also says that the sender is trapped near a bend in the river. Nikki knows it's dangerous, but she has to try to help. She paddles her canoe downriver, coming closer to the thick black smoke of the forest fire with each stroke. When she reaches the bend, Nikki climbs onshore. There, covered with soot and huddled on a rock ledge, sit two small children.

Nikki struggles to get the children to safety. Flames roar around them. Trees splinter to the ground. But as Nikki tries to escape the fire, she doesn't know that two poachers are also hot on her trail. They fear that she and the children have seen too much of their illegal operation—and they'll do anything to keep the kids from making it back to the lodge alive.

The Rock Jockeys

Devil's Wall.

Rick Williams and his friends J.D. and Spud—the Rock Jockeys—are attempting to become the first and youngest climbers to ascend the north face of their area's most treacherous mountain. They're also out to discover if a B-17 bomber rumored to have crashed into the mountain years ago is really there.

As the Rock Jockeys explore Devil's Wall, they stumble upon the plane's battered shell. Inside, they find items that seem to have belonged to the crew, including a diary written by the navigator. Spud later falls into a deep hole and finds something even more frightening: a human skull and bones. To find out where they might have come from, the boys read the navigator's story in the diary. It reveals a gruesome secret that heightens the dangers the mountain might hold for the Rock Jockeys.

Hook 'Em, Snotty

Bobbie Walker loves working on her grandfather's ranch. She hates the fact that her cousin Alex is coming up from Los Angeles to visit and will probably ruin her summer. Alex can barely ride a horse and doesn't know the first thing about roping. There is no way Alex can survive a ride into the flats to round up wild cattle. But Bobbie is going to have to let her tag along anyway.

Out in the flats the weather turns bad. Even worse, Bobbie knows that she'll have to watch out for the Bledsoe boys, two mischievous brothers who are usually up to no good. When the boys rustle the girls' cattle, Bobbie and Alex team up to teach the Bledsoes a lesson. But with the wild bull Diablo on the loose, the fun and games may soon turn deadly serious.

Danger on Midnight River

Daniel Martin doesn't want to go to Camp Eagle Nest. He wants to spend the summer as he always does: with his Uncle Smitty in the Rocky Mountains. Daniel is a slow learner, but most kids call him retarded. Daniel knows that at camp things are only going to get worse. His nightmare comes true when he and three bullies must ride the camp van together.

On the trip to camp Daniel is the butt of the bullies' jokes. He ignores them and concentrates on the roads outside. He thinks they may be lost. As the van crosses a wooden bridge, the planks suddenly give way. The van plunges into the raging river below. Daniel struggles to shore, but the driver and the other boys are nowhere to be found. It's freezing, and night is setting in. Daniel faces a difficult decision. He could save himself . . . or risk everything to try to rescue the others, too.

The Gorgon Slayer

Eleven-year-old Warren Trumbull has a strange job. He works for Prince Charming's Damsel in Distress Rescue Agency, saving people from hideous monsters, evil warlocks, and wicked witches. Then one day Warren gets the most dangerous assignment of all: He must exterminate a Gorgon.

Gorgons are horrible creatures. They have green scales, clawed fingers, and snakes for hair. They also have the power to turn people to stone. Warren doesn't want to be a stone statue for the rest of his life. He'll need all his courage and skill—and his secret plan—to become a true Gorgon slayer.

The Gorgon howls as Warren enters the dark basement to do battle. Warren lowers his eyes, raises his sword and shield, and leaps into action. But will his plan work?